Katie for President

BY MARTHA TOLLES
Illustrated by Ingrid Fetz

SCHOLASTIC INC.
New York Toronto London Auckland Sydney Tokyo

Another book by the author available from Scholastic Inc.:

Katie and Those Boys

To Cindy

ISBN 0-590-10270-2

14 13 12 11 10 9 8 7 6 5   4 5 6 7 8 9/8

Printed in the U.S.A.   01

Contents

The Telephone Call

▲▲▲

It was Saturday morning and Katie Hart was waiting for her brother Dick to drive her to the shopping center. He would be out front any minute, honking the horn for her. But just as she was reaching for the front door, the telephone rang. She ran back to answer it.

"Katie!" It was her best friend, Sarah Lou. "Listen, we're all over here at my house — Jody and Mary and Diane. And we just had a great idea!" Sarah Lou's voice was high with excitement.

"What is it?" Katie sat down on the chair next to the phone and wished, for the umpteenth time, that she didn't live so far away from all her friends. Except for Jo Ann Wentworth, who had lived next door for a few months last year, Katie had always been the only girl in a neighborhood of boys.

Sarah Lou's voice was crackling with excitement. "You remember we were talking about Lynne Colby running for class president?"

"Yes." Katie remembered.

"Well, we want you to run against her."

"Me? Run against Lynne Colby! Oh, I couldn't!"

"Yes, you *could*," Sarah Lou insisted. "We think you're the only one who can beat that Elm Garden crowd. If they win they'll try to run the whole seventh grade."

"Yes, I know but —" Katie was overwhelmed. "But why me? One of you could do it."

"No, we couldn't. You're the best one. Diane is too new here. Jody says she'll have enough to do with the homework in junior high, and Mary's mother wouldn't let her. And I could never do it —"

Diane's voice came over the phone then. "Katie, someone has to stop those Elm Garden girls. They think they're so great. You're the only one who could beat them."

Katie's mind whirled. Could she really run for president? She stared at herself in the hall mirror above the telephone table. Her hazel eyes stared back, serious and, maybe, a little scared. Katie had talked about the election with her friends lots of times, but she never dreamed of running, herself. That was for somebody else.

"Listen." Katie shifted the receiver to her other ear. "You know Lynne Colby. She'll win for sure." Katie heard the front door crash open behind her.

"Katie, come on! Dick says hurry up!" It was her younger brother, Jamie.

Katie motioned him back, at the same time nodding yes to him. "Lynne knows so many kids," she continued, "all the Elm Garden gang. And she's almost eleven months older than I am. Besides she was president of her school last year. They say she's even got a boyfriend...somebody she met at camp this summer."

There was silence at the other end of the phone. Now, Katie thought, they would realize what a crazy idea it was for her to run against Lynne Colby.

"Well, we know it will be tough," Diane admitted. "That's why we want you to try it."

"Suppose some boy runs," Katie said.

"Well, that could happen," Diane conceded.

"You could still run. A three-way race might even be better." That was Sarah Lou again. "Come on, Katie, say you will." Their voices were pleading with her, but the car horn outside sounded impatient.

"I have to go now. Dick's waiting for me. Mom said I can buy my new coat today."

"Well, think about it," her friends said in a chorus.

Katie laughed. "Okay, and thanks for asking me."

As she hung up the phone, she looked at herself again in the mirror — soft hazel eyes in a thin serious face, long brown hair...This was Katie Hart — maybe the next president of the seventh grade. Oh, wow! Could she do it?

Grabbing up her bag, Katie started for the door. "Bye, Mom," she called up the stairs.

Katie's mother was expecting a baby in about a month. She had just caught the flu and the doctor had ordered her to stay in bed until she was well again. She lay there bulky under the covers, propped up against the pillows. "Good-bye Katie," she called down the stairs. "Pick a good coat and don't forget — you need some *sensible* shoes."

When Katie opened the front door, a familiar sight met her eyes. Her brother's old convertible, which he had painted red and black, was jammed with half the boys in the neighborhood. Red-headed Will Madison from next door was in the front seat with Dick and Chuck Miller, the boy

who had moved in when the Wentworths moved out. And, of course, Dick's best friend, Bob Potter, was there with his Irish setter, Red.

Katie smiled to herself. This was the way it had always been here in her neighborhood. Always lots of boys.

"Let's go, Katie," Dick called. "We've got a lot to do."

"Yeah, come on, Katie," Jamie yelled from the back seat. "You're keeping George waiting too." Jamie had a pet garter snake which he kept in a large shoe box when he traveled. He held up the box for Katie to see. Snakes, frogs, and toads were Jamie's favorite pets.

Oh, no! Not the snake too. Well, at least Jamie wouldn't be going shopping with her. Katie hurried out to the car, greeted the boys, and squeezed in back next to her little brother.

"Sorry. I was talking to Sarah Lou. Where are you going?"

Will Madison twisted around in his seat and grinned at Katie. "To Angotti's Dress Shop," he said. "Want us to come in with you?"

Katie usually tried to ignore Will Madison. But today she was so excited about her talk with Sarah Lou that she smiled at his joke.

"We have to take Red to the vet for shots," Dick explained, "and then I have to stop by the drugstore for Mom before I pick you up again."

6

Dick was proud of his car; he'd worked on it for a long time before he got it to go. It was handy too. Since the Harts lived on the edge of town, a couple of miles from the center, Dick often dropped Katie and Jamie off at school, or drove his mother to the supermarket when their father took the family car to work.

They turned onto the busy highway. Other cars began passing them, and the people turned to smile as they passed the crowded convertible. Well, thought Katie, we probably do look sort of funny, with the dog and all.

As Katie stared out the window she thought again about what Sarah Lou and her other friends had asked her on the phone. Class president! They had asked her to run! But should she? Would she dare?

"Dick." Katie leaned forward suddenly. "Do you think I ought to run for president of the seventh grade?"

"Sure, Katie," Dick said over his shoulder. "You'd be good."

"I think so too," Miller agreed.

"Me, too," Bob Potter said. Red chose that moment to lick Katie's cheek.

She hugged the dog and put her cheek against his silky coat. "Do you think any of the boys are going to run?" she asked Will.

Will Madison was in the seventh grade too.

7

"No, it's more fun to play football," he said. "Who are the other girls running for office?"

"They say Lynne Colby." Katie wondered what Will thought of her chances of beating Lynne Colby.

"Is she popular?" Dick asked.

"Yeah, she is," Will answered. "She's got a lot of friends."

"Well, try it, anyway," Dick said, turning into the shopping center. He drove up to Miss Angotti's Dress Shop and Katie climbed out of the car. Most of the kids Katie knew got their clothes at Miss Angotti's.

"Thanks, Dick. See you later." Before she went into the dress shop, Katie hurried into the shoe store next door. She wanted to be ready when the boys came back for her at twelve. But the shoe store was crowded and it took a while before a salesman came to wait on her. She tried on some bright-colored sandals but remembered what her mother had said and finally bought a pair of "sensible" shoes.

By the time Katie entered Miss Angotti's shop it was almost eleven-thirty — not much time left to choose a coat.

A Bad Time in the Dress Shop

▲▲

"I want to buy a winter coat," Katie explained to the dark-haired, plump proprietor of Angotti's Dress Shop.

"How nice." Miss Angotti smiled and raised her thin eyebrows. "Let's see now..." She led Katie over to a rack of coats in the center of the shop. "You wear size seven, don't you? Oh, five? Well, would you like one of these?" she asked, then started holding up coats — one after another — for Katie to examine.

Katie liked a short green coat that she could wear with skirts and jeans, but Miss Angotti favored a full-length red one. "Try this on," she

9

said. "I think you'll like it." Katie put on the red coat to be polite.

Just then the shop door opened and several people crowded through the oblong square of sunshine from the street. Their voices filled the shop and Miss Angotti hurried off to greet the new customers. When she had gone, Katie took off the red coat and hung it back in the rack.

A familiar voice caught her ear. She glanced around to see Lynne Colby with a group of her friends and a woman Katie thought must be Mrs. Colby. The Elm Garden crowd! What a coincidence! Katie pushed the coats on the rack apart and watched the Colbys through the opening. Lynne was looking through a rack of dresses and her mother was saying something about pleats and darts. Katie looked at the red coat and wondered with sudden longing what *her* mother would say about pleats and darts. But there was no shopping with Mom today.

Lynne certainly was good looking, Katie thought, with her dark eyes and long dark hair. When she came out of the dressing room in a bright yellow dress, she posed for her friends. They gathered around her in an admiring circle. That was the thing about Lynne Colby. She always had a large crowd of friends with her. She seemed so much older than Katie and her friends, and so sure of herself. Katie noticed that Lynne was wearing sandals with sheer panty hose. Katie and her friends still wore knee socks or thick cotton panty hose with skirts — or blue jeans. Lynne never wore jeans.

Unconsciously Katie glanced at herself in the full-length mirror. She saw an average-sized girl, a little thin, in a skirt, sweater, and knee socks. There was nothing special about her. How could she have the nerve to run against someone like Lynne Colby in the school election?

Katie realized suddenly that she had better get busy and choose a coat. The boys would be coming to pick her up any minute. Miss Angotti returned to her again.

"Here are some other coats..." she was saying, when she was interrupted by the familiar beep of a horn. Through the glass on the front door Katie could see Dick's car pulling up in front of the store. All the boys were still in the car and all their faces, including the dog's, were turned toward the dress shop. And all the faces in the dress shop were turned toward them. Katie heard one of the girls say, "Look at that car, would you?"

"Oh, no!" Katie exclaimed. Jamie was getting out of the car — with the shoe box.

"I'll take the green coat," she said quickly digging in her bag for the money. She had to get out

11

before Jamie came in. This wasn't the place for a snake.

Miss Angotti surrendered the green coat and began to wrap it up. Katie hurried to the door, hoping to get there before Jamie. But Lynne and her friend were standing in the way. "Excuse me," she said, trying to get past them.

One of the girls turned to her. "Are they waiting for you?" She motioned to the car.

"Yes," Katie nodded.

"Are they your brothers?" Lynne asked.

Katie tried to squeeze past the girls. "Two of them are." But it was too late — the door of the shop flew open and Jamie was inside.

"Katie," Jamie shouted. "We're here. Want to see some great worms I got for George? He really likes them."

"George!" One of the girls laughed. "Worms!"

"Sure, George." Jamie was beaming. Before Katie could stop him he had pulled the lid off the box. "See? There he is!"

"Oh-h-h-h!" The girls screamed this time. "Look out, a snake!"

In their haste to get away, they knocked the shoe box out of Jamie's hands and George was dumped on the carpet.

Jamie dived to the floor, but George was already slithering away — heading toward Miss Angotti.

"Help!" Miss Angotti skipped behind a waste-paper basket. "Take that terrible thing out of my store!" she ordered in a high, quavering voice. George disappeared under a rack of dresses.

"Jamie, get him!" Katie cried. "Oh, this is awful!"

Jamie dove right through the dresses, so that the whole rack came crashing down on top of him.

"Oh, Jamie! Are you hurt?" Katie rushed over to him.

"George!" Jamie's muffled voice could be heard as he thrashed around in the dresses.

"Good gracious," Mrs. Colby exclaimed.

"Help me catch him," Katie called to the girls.

"Uh-uh. I don't want to touch him," Lynne said, backing away with her friends.

Katie dropped to her knees. She had to help Jamie. He was crazy about George. But for one second she thought this must be a terrible nightmare. She wasn't really down on the floor chasing a snake in Miss Angotti's shop, with Lynne Colby and her friends watching! This really couldn't be happening to her, could it?

"Katie," said Jamie, who had finally pulled himself clear of the pile of dresses, "don't let anybody step on him."

Katie moved cautiously. Ah, there he was! She inched forward — then swooped. She had him at

13

last. She rose to her feet, her hair hanging in her face, George wrapped around her wrist. Lynne and her friends drew farther back — laughing now.

Miss Angotti rushed toward Katie, a stream of angry words pouring from her lips. Jamie darted forward with the shoe box and Katie found herself and Jamie and George being hustled out of Angotti's Dress Shop. A plastic coat bag was handed to her out the door. "And your coat," Miss Angotti said sharply, closing the door.

Jamie hugged her. "Oh, thank you, Katie, thank you."

"It's okay," Katie sighed, knowing she'd made *him* happy anyway. It was about the most embarrassing experience she'd ever had in her life.

"What took you so long?" Dick asked, impatiently gunning the motor.

"Katie was probably showing George to Lynne Colby and her crowd." Will's blue eyes were bright with laughter.

Katie sank onto the back seat, ignoring Will's teasing. "Just everything happened," she sighed. Lynne and her bunch would be laughing at her forever now. Could anyone ever think of her as class president? Oh, why did it have to happen?

14

A Fire at School

▲▲

Katie worried all weekend about whether she should run for president. Her mother said, "Yes, by all means. You should take part in school activities." And Sarah Lou must have called at least six times to talk about it. But the thought of running against Lynne Colby was chilling.

On Monday Katie was still debating with herself. She had almost decided to run...but not quite. As she was going up the school steps after lunch she met Maria Sanches, a small, dark-haired girl from Mexico City, who had just started at Katie's school this year.

"Hi, Maria." Katie stopped to talk. She thought she knew how it must feel to be in a new country, in a new school, with new friends. "How's everything going?" Katie asked. "Is your locker all right?" She had helped Maria with the combination on her locker the first day of school.

"Everything is okay, Katie." Maria's dark eyes brightened at the sight of Katie. "But I have much work to do. I wish I knew how to do it better. This school is very different." As Maria talked on about her school work, Katie noticed that Lynne and her friends were standing nearby. They would glance over their shoulders at Maria, obviously listening to her conversation, then turn back to each other. Little smiles flitted from face to face, superior smiles that seemed to say: listen to that strange new girl. Then one of the girls said something and they all laughed, throwing sideways glances at Maria. Katie began to feel a burning sensation deep down inside. What was so funny anyway?

Fortunately Maria had her back to Lynne's crowd and hadn't seen them. "And, Katie," she was saying, "I hear something good. Sarah Lou says you might be class president."

"Oh, Maria, I haven't even decided to run, yet." *Haven't you?* a voice inside her asked. And then something clicked in her mind. If that was the way Lynne Colby and her friends were going to act...if that was how they were going to treat a new girl...then someone ought to run against them.

Katie looked at Maria. "Well, maybe I will run. Yes, I *am*. I'm going to try for it!"

And so she had made up her mind at last! Her friends would be pleased, she knew.

Before the start of English class that afternoon, the teacher, Mrs. Carson, asked Katie to deliver a notice to each of the seventh grade classrooms. Katie wished she could make the announcement as she went from room to room: "I'm going to run for class president."

When she came to Will Madison's class, he waved to her from the back of the room, stuck out his tongue, and rolled his eyes. Katie, pretending not to see him, stuck her nose in the air. But the awful part was that he made her want to laugh. That Will Madison!

Back in the hall, she went to the door of the science room. Was she supposed to deliver a notice in there? She wasn't sure, so she pushed the door open slowly.

What a scene! It was like opening the door onto a movie — a terrible, frightening movie! Dark smoke swirled about the room; orange flames flared up from a wastebasket and licked at the end of a lab counter. Katie stared in horror. The acrid burning smell caught in her throat and she knew this was real. "Fire! Fire!" she shouted. Her eyes were stinging from the smoke. She whirled around,

17

got out of the room, and shut the door. Quick! She must get help, fast!

Her feet pounded down the hall, past the closed classrooms, past the staring faces. She flung herself through the door of the principal's office. "Fire!" she shouted into the startled face of his secretary. "Fire in the science room!"

"Wha-a-a-at?" The secretary dropped the papers she was holding. Mr. Barker, the principal, was not in his office.

"Quick, call the fire department!" Katie yelled.

The woman grabbed the phone and began to dial. Just then Mr. Barker burst through the office door. "Fire!" he and his secretary shouted at each other. Then there were running feet, high voices, and the fire alarm began to blast through the school like a hoarse cry. Someone took Katie by the shoulders and pushed her into the hall. "Get in line!" a voice commanded her. Already lines of students were filing through the corridors, faces serious, eyes frightened.

Katie had closed the science room door, but dark smoke and the bitter smell had seeped into the hall. Katie hurried along with the other students, as the fire alarm continued its short, tense blasts. No one talked. Everyone moved quickly down the hall, around the corner, and at last outdoors. It felt good to gulp the crisp clean air and move away from the building.

The smell of burning was stronger outside, and off in the distance came the shrill cry of a siren, shrieking closer and closer. Katie spotted Sarah Lou and slipped over to her. "Isn't it awful?" she whispered.

Sarah Lou nodded, her eyes serious. "I wonder how it happened?"

"I don't know, but I was delivering notices for Mrs. Carson, and I went in there — in the science room, I mean. I saw the smoke and flames!" Would she ever forget that frightening scene in the quiet room? Her legs still felt shaky.

"*You* gave the alarm, Katie?" Sarah Lou stared at her.

A fire engine raced into the parking lot, its siren down to a low growl. Men leaped off the truck, rolling out a thick fire hose. The students began to push forward to watch the firemen as they disappeared inside the long, low stucco school building. Katie could hear everyone around her beginning to talk and ask questions. Only the blackbirds on the school lawn seemed not to care, and continued picking at the ground.

The fire was under control quickly and the long blast of the all-clear signal was soon sounded.

"Hey, Katie," one of the boys whispered to her as their line began to move back into school. "You were in there. How'd it happen? Who started it?"

Katie shrugged. "I don't know."

20

Back in the classroom, Mrs. Carson rapped sharply for order. "Let's forget the fire now. We've lost a lot of time," she said. But that was an impossible request. Every time the teacher turned her back, someone whispered, "Katie, did you see anything?" But Katie could only shake her head.

There was a sudden rumble of static from the loudspeaker on the wall and the voice of Mr. Barker came over the school intercom. "Boys and girls, I know you are all wondering about the fire in the science room. Fortunately, it was discovered quickly by one of our students before it could go too far. But I regret to say that it did cause some serious damage to one of the lab tables."

Then he said, "We will get to the bottom of this. But in the meantime, let's all get back to work." He sounded worried and no wonder! The high school had been plagued with trash-can fires last year, and now it seemed to be starting in junior high. It wasn't a good beginning for the year.

After class, as Katie rose to leave, Mrs. Carson beckoned to her. "Mr. Barker would like to see you after school, Katie," she said.

Katie felt a moment of worry. Surely he didn't think she had anything to do with it — anything like that. She tried not to worry about it during the rest of her classes, but the news had spread. All the other students knew now that she had discovered the fire, and they kept asking her about it:

21

What was it like? How did it get started? Who did it?

As soon as classes were over, Katie went straight to Mr. Barker's office. The secretary motioned her into the inner office, where Mr. Barker was sitting at his desk.

Everything about Mr. Barker was gray, Katie decided as she sat down. Gray eyes, gray at the edges of his hair, a gray suit. And now there were gray lines in his face. When he smiled he looked quite different, but there was no smiling now.

"Hello, Katie. We certainly appreciated your quick alarm this afternoon. Now tell me, did you see anything or any*one* in the science room? Anything at all?"

Katie frowned. She could only tell him what she had told everyone else. All she saw were the bright flames and the black smoke. She'd never forget that.

"No, Mr. Barker, I just saw the fire. That's all. It was terrible!" It made her shiver to think of it again.

"Well, that's all right, Katie. You were a great help. We have to ask these questions, you see. Thanks for coming in to talk to me." He nodded to her, and then picked up the telephone.

Katie left the office with a feeling of relief. So that was all Mr. Barker wanted. But as she was walking out the office door, Will Madison came around the corner. His blue eyes lighted up like candles when he saw her. "Hey, where've you been, Katie?"

"Nowhere much." Even though she hadn't done anything wrong, she didn't feel like telling Will she'd been called to the office, while all the other students were crowding past them.

"Got called to the office, huh?" he guessed. "Are you in trouble?" She wished he didn't have such a loud voice.

"Of course not!" Why did he think that?

His blue eyes teased her. "Say, I get it. You were called in for starting the fire. Good old Katie, in trouble at last!"

"Will Madison! You know I didn't start that fire! Don't even say such a thing."

Katie could feel her face getting hot and, to make things worse, she noticed that Lynne's friend, Sheryl, had come up behind Will and was listening. Katie could tell by that nosy look on her face. She made Katie even more upset.

"Mr. Barker just wanted to know if I'd seen anything. That's all." Katie hurried away to her locker, leaving Will's teasing face and Sheryl's questioning eyes behind her.

A Whistle in Assembly

No one confessed to starting the fire. A Bunsen burner had been found tipped over on the lab counter, and so it looked as though someone had been working in the lab without supervision. That was against the rules, as Mr. Barker pointed out on the school intercom, and he again urged the culprit to come in and confess. "It would be the best thing to do," he said.

Then it was Thursday, the day before assembly, when the nominations for class office were to be made. Katie and her friends went to Sarah Lou's house after school that day to make their plans. They gathered around the kitchen table for cookies and milk.

"I wonder if any boys are going to run?" Katie frowned a little, sliding glasses around the table to everyone.

"I heard they're not." Diane poured milk into her glass.

"Oh, wow! Just the two of us?" Katie stared at Diane for a moment. "I wonder how Lynne is going to like that." She was silent for a minute and then said, "Wouldn't it really be better if one of you tried out for it instead of me? The fire and all the questions..." Katie looked around at her friends.

"The fire! You saved us by finding it in time, remember?"

"Katie, we've been all through this. You're the best choice all around." Sarah Lou opened a box of cookies. "Diane's a newcomer. Jody and I have no experience, and Mary —"

"Not me!" Mary put in. "The work's too hard at school. My mother wouldn't let me."

Katie smiled. They were determined she should do it. "Well, okay. Someone will have to nominate me, then. How about you, Sarah Lou, since you've known me the longest. And Diane, you could second it?"

"Okay," Diane agreed. "What are you going to say in your speech?"

"She's had experience as a leader," Sarah Lou pointed out. "She was president of the fourth

grade. And she was in charge of Play Day in fifth."
Sarah Lou was nibbling on her third cookie. She was always worrying about her weight, but she liked to eat.

"Katie's used to standing up for things," Diane said, pulling at her short, dark hair thoughtfully. "I mean, any girl who's grown up with all those boys — well, she'd know how to get along." Diane lived only a block away from the school and was always saying how she wished she could ride back and forth to school in Dick's car. "Besides," she continued, "maybe a lot of the boys will vote for Katie, especially if no boy runs for it."

Jody looked around at the others. "I sure hope we can beat that Elm Garden gang," she said. "They're so stuck-up!"

"They don't even say hello," Mary added. "But they pay plenty of attention to the boys."

"They all wear nylon panty hose to school too." Sarah Lou looked wistful. "And bras."

"Maybe we should, too. I mean..." Jody looked self-conscious. "Anybody can *wear* things."

"My mother says she's not going to waste money before she has to," Sarah Lou sighed.

"I hate nylon panty hose," Diane declared. "You can't do anything in them without getting a run."

"It would be kind of fun though." Katie said,

26

glancing down at her jeans. But she knew her family was saving money for the new baby. "Well, listen, I ought to have some posters...."

They decided then to make some posters with the slogan, You Gotta Have Hart! That was Sarah Lou's idea.

"But what shall I say in assembly tomorrow?" Katie asked.

"Tell them what we were just saying," Diane urged. "You know, about being president of the fourth grade, and how you can get along with boys."

"That's not going to be easy," Katie pointed out.

She knew she was going to worry about her speech, and she did — all evening, and the next day. What should she say in assembly? By late afternoon, when the entire seventh grade had filed into the auditorium, Katie couldn't remember ever feeling more nervous. Her hands felt sticky, her throat felt dry, and she was sure her hair needed brushing. Would her yellow sweater and her best corduroy skirt look all right? Up until today the elections and nominations hadn't seemed quite real. But now they were! And now Lynne would find out for sure that Katie was running against her. How would she like that?

Katie sat with her friends in a row of seats about halfway down the aisle. An eighth grade boy, Mike Cooper, was in charge of the meeting. He spoke into a microphone up on the stage, and after a very brief introduction he called for nominations for president. Sheryl was on her feet at once. "I nominate Lynne Colby," she said in a clear, assured voice.

Another friend, Elizabeth, stood up beside her. "I second the nomination."

Mike repeated the nomination over the microphone and asked Lynne to come up to the stage. She was wearing a brilliant blue skirt and sweater, and she looked at least sixteen. She walked across the stage to the speaker's stand and leaned toward the microphone. She didn't look a bit nervous. She smoothed back her hair and began to talk in a low, calm voice. She said she had always had a good record at school, both in grades and citizenship. She had held class office every year since third grade. Last year she was president of her school, and she even mentioned that she had traveled "widely" during summer vacations. She said she would attend every student government meeting before school on Fridays.

Katie almost felt herself getting smaller and smaller. No wonder Lynne acted so important. She was! Katie wished she'd never gotten into this whole business. As Lynne walked back to her seat, the students clapped loudly for her.

Then Mike was calling for the next nomination. Sarah Lou was on her feet. Just what she said, Katie wasn't sure, for her mind was going around in frightened circles. What was it she had planned to say? Should she even bother? She'd probably only get about six votes out of the class of three hundred.

Katie searched the front row, looking for Lynne. There she was, glancing back over the auditorium, her dark hair thrown back, her face curious as if she were trying to figure out why this Katie Hart had dared oppose her.

"Get up, Katie." Sarah Lou poked her. Katie rose on shaking legs, wishing she were a thousand miles away. She could see her friends smiling at her, as she started down the aisle.

The stage looked high and far away. Yet she found herself up there and talking into the microphone in no time at all. She even remembered the speech she had prepared. She listed her activities and then, what was she saying? Something about living in a neighborhood of boys, and how the president of the class had usually been a boy in the past, but because she was used to boys... At last, she was saying thank you and starting for her seat.

A sprinkling of clapping began as she came

down the steps from the stage. Then all of a sudden a loud, clear whistle pierced the air — then another, and another. Katie was so startled she slipped on the edge of one of the steps and skidded wildly, almost losing her balance. A huge laugh welled up and up, sweeping across the auditorium, drowning her with its noise. Every face turned toward her was grinning. Somehow Katie made her way up the aisle, past all the laughing faces. She sank down into her seat, hot all over with embarrassment.

"Who did that?" Katie hissed fiercely at Sarah Lou.

"Quiet, please!" Mike was rapping on the table up front. But even he had a big grin on his face. The laughing and talking continued, and he had to call again for order. There was a moment's quiet while everyone waited for more nominations for president, but there were none. So no boys were going to run! Katie shivered a little, realizing that she was the only one running against Lynne Colby. Other nominations followed: a boy and a girl for vice-president, another boy named Jeff for treasurer, and two girls for secretary. They all received a big round of applause, although none as great as Lynne's.

When assembly was over and the students were crowding down the aisles, many of them looked over and grinned at Katie. "I'd like to know who started that whistling," Katie muttered.

"Never mind, Katie," Diane sympathized.

"Did you see how surprised Lynne looked when I nominated you?" Sarah Lou exclaimed.

"Yeah, but now we've got to figure out how to beat her," Jody pointed out. "She's got a lot of friends."

"Congratulations, Katie!" That came from several girls squeezing past them in the aisle. Maria, too, called out: "Good for you, Katie. I will vote for you."

"Thanks, Maria." Katie was just beginning to feel better when, "Well, well," a voice teased behind her. "Look who's running for president!"

"Get lost, Will!" Sarah Lou said.

"Watch out," Diane warned. "He's one vote, and he has friends."

"You hear that, Katie?" Will poked her. There was a big smile on his face. "You'd better be nice to me." And through his teeth he blew an echo of that louder, earlier whistle.

"Will Madison," Katie burst out. "Did you do that?"

Will just grinned and moved off through the crowd. Katie glared after him. "I should have known. Sarah Lou, did you hear that?"

Sarah Lou nodded. "Forget about him, Katie."

As they passed out of the auditorium, Katie saw Lynne with a large group of friends gathered around her. Most of them turned to give Katie a searching glance. Then they huddled together, whispering, until the whole group burst into laughter. Were they laughing at *her*? Katie hurried past. To her horror, she felt tears stinging under her eyelids. Why, with all those friends and Lynne so used to running things...and Will going around whistling and making her feel silly...well, of course Lynne would win.

The Only One

▲▲

Katie and Sarah Lou stood looking at the campaign posters on the bulletin board in the school hall. Katie had tacked hers up yesterday; Lynne must have put hers up that morning.

"Oh, Sarah Lou, look how good hers is!" Katie cried. A sense of defeat came over her again. The poster had a painted gold border, and in the middle was an 8x10 color photograph of Lynne. Above the photograph, in beautiful gold lettering, it said: "Vote for Lynne Colby." That was all. Simple, but impressive.

"Katie, yours is okay. It's different, that's all."

"It looks like a little kid's." Katie was disgusted. She frowned at the red lettering: "You Gotta

33

Have Hart." The red hearts at the bottom had been colored with red crayon. "It looks so...so bad," Katie muttered.

"But yours is sort of humorous. Hers is serious. It's just like Lynne to make a big deal out of herself."

Katie smiled at Sarah Lou. She always tried to make you feel better. Still, Katie wished she could take down the poster and do another. But that would be worse. Lynne and her friends would probably make some nasty comments.

That day didn't get any better. In the afternoon when she got home, Katie called to her mother, but no answering voice came floating back to her. Perhaps Mom was taking a nap. Katie went upstairs quietly and pushed open her parents' bedroom door.

The bed was empty and the yellow bedspread had been pulled over it. In the center of the bed was a note. "Mom!" Katie darted forward and threw herself down on the bed. For a minute she didn't read the note. She buried her face in the bedspread. Then she picked up the note and read: "Dear Katie, It's time now. Dad is taking me to the hospital. Please take care of Jamie. Love, Mother."

Katie put down the note slowly. Gone now were all thoughts of Lynne and posters. Who cared

34

about all that? Mom had gone to have the baby. Would she be all right? What would the baby be like?

Jamie burst open the door, and stood staring at the bed. "Where's Mom?"

"She went to the hospital, Jamie, to have the baby."

"Oh, no!" Jamie scowled. "I don't want that old baby."

"It's okay, Jamie." Katie's own scary thoughts retreated. How silly of her! Of course everything would be all right.

Jamie came over and sat on the bed. "I don't want Mom to go to the hospital."

Katie put her arms around him and gave him a hug. "It'll only be for a few days. Besides, Jamie—" she searched for something to cheer him up, "the baby will think you're really great, you know."

"He will?" Jamie looked at Katie with interest. "Why?"

"Well, look at all the things you can do that he can't." Katie decided to go along with Jamie's choice of "he." "You can walk and talk and run. He won't be able to do any of those things."

"Say, that's right." A satisfied smile spread over his face, and he got up and paced around the room with great long steps.

Katie had to laugh. "Let's go down and get

something to eat now," she suggested.

When Jamie had settled himself in front of the television set in the den with milk and cookies, Katie went outside to find Dick. His car was parked in the driveway, and his legs were sticking out from underneath the engine.

"Dick." Katie rushed toward him. "Did you know Mom's gone to the hospital?"

"Yeah, I know." Dick's voice came from underneath the car.

"Do you think — uh — everything will be okay?"

"Sure." His voice sounded muffled, as though he had something in his mouth. "Hope it's a boy." She knew he was saying that to tease her, but she was used to it now. She decided to stay out there with him. She got into the car and listened to him tinkering around.

She tried to remember where her old dolls were, just in case... and her old blue-and-white tea set. It ought to be a girl. There were so many boys around here already. Besides, didn't she have two brothers? Katie began to daydream. The baby *would* be a girl and somehow, she didn't know just how, she would win the election. She could see herself up in front of the assembly, everyone clapping...

* * *

It seemed as though they waited for hours that evening for news from the hospital. When the phone finally rang, Katie rushed to answer it. "Dad! What's happening?"

"Your mother's going to have a baby — sometime."

"Oh, Dad!" How could he make jokes now? "Is Mom okay?"

"She's fine," he assured her. "When I have some news I'll call you. Otherwise, I'll see you in the morning. There's nothing to worry about."

But as Katie got ready for bed and put on her long granny nightgown, she began to get that uneasy feeling again. She was sure she would never get to sleep. She slid into bed and stared out the window at a cold moon, high in the dark sky. Would her mom really be all right?

Worrisome thoughts about her mother kept pushing into her mind. Would there be a lot of pain? Would she cry? She hated to think about her mother hurting. Then a wonderfully comforting thought occurred to her. Mom had had other babies — three of them. She'd be all right this time too.

It was morning when Katie awakened. Bright yellow sunlight streamed through the white curtains onto her flowered wallpaper. For a moment she couldn't think why she had an uneasy feeling.

Then it came to her. Mom! Did she have the baby yet?

Suddenly she heard a voice downstairs. It was her father! He was back! Katie threw off the covers and leaped out of bed. She ran to the door. "Dad!" There was a strong smell of coffee in the air and from the head of the stairs she could hear sounds in the kitchen. Holding up her nightgown, she raced downstairs. All fear vanished. Of course Mom was all right or Dad wouldn't be downstairs in the kitchen drinking coffee.

"Dad!" She stopped in the doorway. There he was, leaning back in his chair, a cigar in his mouth — she'd never seen him smoke a cigar — and a smile spread across his face like a banner. "Oh, Dad! How's Mom?"

"Fine, fine." Her father waved his smelly cigar. "Never been better. She's sleeping right now."

"Oh, I'm so glad!" Katie flopped down in a chair. "And, Dad... is the baby..." She couldn't finish the question.

"The baby is fine too, Katie," her dad added. "A healthy nine-pound boy. We've named him Pete."

"Oh! a boy." Katie choked back her disappointment. Her eyes blurred as she stared down at the table.

"Katie," her father said gently, "come over here

and sit on my lap." Katie frowned, staring at the table.

"I'm too big to sit on people's laps anymore."

"I know." Her father pushed aside his coffee and put down his cigar. "But I don't have any little girls. You are my only one."

"Oh, Dad." Katie lurched out of her chair and threw herself into her father's arms. For a moment the tears came. Maybe some of it was plain relief after the waiting. Her father's voice rumbled next to her ear while he patted her shoulder. "There, there."

Katie sat for a moment longer while her father talked about Mom and how she was doing. Then he said, "I think I'm going to need neck surgery if you don't move your head pretty soon."

"Oh, sorry, Dad." Katie laughed and struggled up out of his lap. She felt suddenly hungry. "Shall I fix you some eggs now?" She went over to the refrigerator.

"Certainly, I'd like that...breakfast with my only daughter." Katie had the strangest thought then: Would I mind if there were a new little girl in the house and she climbed into Dad's lap?

Will Helps Out

▰▰▰

Katie pushed open the door of the den. The TV was muttering away, but Jamie was not there. "Jamie! Jamie!" She went through the silent rooms, calling for him. But there was no answer. He must have gone down to Bobby's, she decided.

How quiet the house was with no one else there. Dick had left early in the morning to work at the Highway Garage. He'd agreed to fill in for a friend who was in a state track meet that day. And after breakfast Dad said he was going to stop by the hospital for a visit, and then go on to his office. That left Katie in charge.

But why hadn't Jamie told her where he was going? He'd been acting really strange lately. If he

got the least bit of a bump or scrape, he'd run upstairs to their parents' room and sit there for the
longest time.

Katie went to the phone and dialed Bobby's
number. It rang and rang but no one answered.
She went to check her parents' room. It was
empty. Then she went to Jamie's room. His room
was a mess, with all the drawers pulled open and
clothes spilled out on the floor. She ran downstairs
and out to the backyard. He wasn't there either.
She hurried out front and scanned all the yards on
the street. For once there was not a single boy in
sight...just the wide street and green lawns with
scattered clumps of yellow and white chrysan-
themums.

She hurried down the street. Maybe they just
hadn't heard the phone at Bobby's house. But no
one answered the doorbell either. Maybe he was
next door at Will's. She ran back up the street.
But Will's backyard was empty too. A wave of fear
swept over Katie. Where was Jamie? She raced into the house and called her father's office. The
phone rang and rang. He hadn't gotten there yet.
What should she do? Certainly she couldn't call
her mother at the hospital. Should she phone the
police? That was a scary idea.

Maybe Will's mother was home. She'd know
what to do. Katie ran out the front door again. She

was just crossing the front lawn to ring the Madisons' doorbell when she saw Will coming down the street on his bike.

"Will!" She rushed toward him. "Can you help me?"

Will skidded to a stop, his blue eyes questioning.

"I can't find Jamie. I've been up and down the whole block." She waved her arms about. "I've been to Bobby's and — and everywhere."

Will's eyes focused on her face as she continued to describe her search. "I don't know how long he's been gone!" She began to feel frantic.

"Maybe he's over on the next street," Will said calmly. "Want me to go look for him?"

"Would you? I'll stay here in case he shows up. He's not supposed to go that far. Maybe he thinks he can get away with it — with just me here."

Will took off on his bike and Katie stood on the curb, looking after him. Will was sure to find Jamie, she told herself. Sometimes she forgot how nice he could be, even if he did whistle at her in assembly.

A few cars passed, but otherwise the street was quiet. Then Will appeared around the corner. He didn't shout or wave, and he wasn't smiling. He didn't have Jamie with him either. A sickening feeling swept over Katie. "You didn't find him?" she said.

"Uh-uh." Will shook his head. He stopped his bike and balanced on one foot. "I talked to this kid over on Walnut." He waved toward the next street. "He claims he saw Jamie."

"He did? When?"

"He said Jamie was walking up Walnut a while back, carrying a suitcase."

"A suitcase?" Katie's mind rushed back to the mess in Jamie's room — the drawers pulled open, clothes yanked out. "But why?"

"He told this kid he was going to the hospital to see his mother."

"The hospital!" Katie was horrified. "Oh, no! He couldn't! It's too far. All those busy streets —"

"He could try."

"I have to find him. He might get lost or — or — run over." Katie threw a frantic glance up and down the street. If only Dick were here. Why would Jamie do such a crazy thing? "Do you think your mother could help?"

Will shook his head. "She's out shopping. But listen, why don't you go get your bike? I'll go with you."

"It's got a flat tire. It'll take too long to fix."

"Well —" Will paused for a second. "Get on mine. Here." Will leaned back, motioning toward the crossbar.

Katie hesitated, but the feeling of fright was almost choking her now. Jamie, her little brother,

43

was gone — with a suitcase — and she was in charge. Yes, the best thing was to go after him.

"Okay. Thanks, Will." She hurried over to him. Will turned the bike around and Katie sat on the crossbar. "Let's hurry," she urged.

He started pedaling. "I hope I'm not too heavy," Katie said, leaning forward on the handle bars so her hair wouldn't blow in his face. It came to her in a rush of embarrassment that she was awfully close to Will Madison. In fact, she didn't dare look around at him.

"It's okay," Will said behind her. "We've got to find Jamie. We'd better cross over to Walnut."

The bike creaked as they rolled along, and the tires swished against the pavement. On Walnut Street, Katie strained her eyes up the long, shaded street. The boy Will had spoken to was nowhere in sight.

"Would Jamie know how to get to the hospital?" Will asked.

"I told him one day," Katie answered over her shoulder. "He was asking me about Mom and about the hospital, and all that. I remember I explained it was up Walnut, across the boulevard, and through Elm Garden."

Will whistled. "Well, we'll catch him. I think."

But would they? How far had he gone? If only she had paid more attention to him this morning.

They reached the heavy traffic on the boulevard and had to wait for the light to change to green. People in their cars no doubt thought that she and Will were just out for a ride — a happy girl in jeans and a T-shirt, and a redheaded, freckle-nosed boy and his bike.

Katie watched nervously as a huge trailer truck rumbled up to the light and stopped with a screeching of brakes. "Do you think Jamie would really cross here?" she asked.

"He could have." Will and Katie wheeled the bike across the street. "But he'd wait for the light." Will assured her. "Jamie's got good sense."

"Well, sometimes," Katie agreed.

They mounted the bike again and started up Walnut Street. Katie asked again if she was too heavy. "Don't worry about it," Will scoffed. "You're not half as bad as Miller."

She was trying to decide whether or not that was a compliment when she saw a crowd of boys and girls up the street. "Will, look. Do you think —" She leaned forward, staring at the figures. None of them had a suitcase.

Will angled the bike over to the group. "Let's ask them."

"Have you seen a little kid with a suitcase?" Katie called out.

A tall boy in a red shirt said he had seen a little kid with a suitcase, but it was quite a while ago.

46

That was both good news and bad. At least they were going in the right direction, but how far ahead of them was Jamie? Where would he go after he left Elm Garden?

Will pedaled off again, and the tall boy shouted after them: "Hey, is that your girl friend?"

Katie and Will rode in embarrassed silence for a minute. Dumb kid, Katie thought. Will was just trying to help her. "At least we know he went this way," she said finally, avoiding any mention of the boy. "It's a long way for Jamie, though."

"Let's hope he gets tired." Will's voice sounded as though he, too, were trying to ignore what the boy had said. Katie longed to look back at him but she didn't dare. Was he annoyed, embarrassed, or maybe pleased? Oh, wow! She couldn't believe it! Here she was so worried about Jamie, and her mind insisted on thinking about the strangest things. Did Will Madison like her? Oh, what a crazy idea!

Will suddenly let out a yelp. "Look who's coming!" Around the corner from a side street came two cyclists, followed by a large Irish setter.

"It's Miller and Bob!" Katie waved, feeling a sudden lift of hope. "And Red. We're looking for Jamie!" she shouted.

"You guys seen him?" Will steered toward them

"No. We were at the park." Miller and Bob circled around them. "Where'd you see him last?"

"He went off with a suitcase." Katie couldn't keep the tremor out of her voice. "We think he's going to the hospital to see Mom," she explained.

"Oh!" Both boys looked startled. "We'll help you look," Miller offered.

"You want to get on my bike for a change, Katie?" Bob grinned at Will.

Maybe Will would like her to get off, she thought. "Do you want a rest, Will?" she asked.

"Naw, I'm not tired," he replied, and started pedaling faster. "Come on, we can't waste time."

"Yes, let's hurry." Katie leaned forward in her eagerness to find Jamie.

The Elm Garden Crowd

▲▲▲

The houses in Elm Garden, a new section of town, were all large, low, and modern. This was where Lynne Colby and her group lived. Walnut Street, which ran straight in the older part of town, began winding through here. As Katie and the boys came around a bend, they saw, up ahead, a small figure sitting by the curb, feet resting on a suitcase, chin in hand. It couldn't be... but it was!

"Jamie!" Katie shrieked, jumping off the bike before Will could stop. Red raced ahead of her, barking and wagging his tail. "Jamie, oh, Jamie!" She rushed toward him. "We've been looking and looking for you. Oh, thank goodness! Jamie Hart, what were you trying to do anyway?"

"I'm sorry, Katie." Jamie hung his head.

"Why did you do such a thing?" She wanted to shake him and hug him at the same time. His brown hair stuck up in the air and his face was smudged. It looked as though he'd been waiting there, hoping she'd come and find him.

Katie's knees were shaking. She sat down suddenly beside her small brother and gave him a hug. He didn't push her away either, so she knew he must be feeling really sorry. "Where were you going?"

Jamie looked at his hands. "The hospital. I — I wanted to see Mom."

"I thought we'd catch up with you." Will leaned over the handlebars of his bike. "You okay, Jamie?" he asked.

"Uh huh." Jamie was still examining his dirty hands. "I guess I got tired. Besides, I — I wasn't sure if this was the way anymore. It's pretty far to the hospital."

"It sure is. I was so scared — " Katie's glance fell on the suitcase and for the first time she noticed George's box. "Jamie, you weren't taking George to the hospital, too?"

"Sure. I have to take George. Mom might want to see him."

Katie couldn't help smiling. "What've you got in your suitcase?"

"Oh, some things." Jamie pulled the case onto his knees and snapped it open, revealing crumpled pajamas, socks, and two model cars.

Katie shook her head. "Jamie, you couldn't stay overnight at the hospital. People have to be sick or having a baby to stay there. Trying to walk all that way...and not telling me..." She started to get that tight feeling in her stomach again.

"Let's go home," Bob suggested.

Jamie stood up. "Yeah, I'm hungry."

"Oh, say, it must be past noon," Katie exclaimed, grabbing at Bob's wrist to look at his watch. "Dad said he'd call at lunchtime. He must be trying to reach me." Katie could almost hear the phone ringing and ringing in the empty house. He would be worried. "I don't know what he's going to think." She frowned, looking about the quiet neighborhood. "Wish I could phone from here."

Will sat back on his bike. "We'd better get going. One of you guys take Jamie."

Katie bent over her tennis shoes, trying to hide the astonishment that must be showing on her face. Did Will want her to ride back with him? Then another thought struck her. Maybe he expected her to walk. Why not? He probably expected her to jog alongside.

Before any of them could start off, however, a

52

car passed them, stopped at a house up the street, and let out a group of girls. It was some of the Elm Garden crowd! — Sheryl and Elizabeth and Lynne.

"Say, maybe Lynne Colby lives over there." Will sat astride his bike, watching. The group of girls went up the walk together and disappeared inside a low pink house. "You could use her phone," he suggested.

"Oh, well — I — I suppose so." Katie didn't really want to go up there and face Lynne and the other girls. But how could she explain that to the boys? And she would have to explain to the girls what she was doing here. Still, she should call her father.

"What's the matter? Scared?" Will's blue eyes were laughing at her.

"Don't be silly!" Katie stood up quickly. It was annoying to think Will had read her mind.

"I'm thirsty." Jamie took her hand. "Can I come?"

Katie looked at her brother. "Well, if you stay outside. They might not want a snake in their house."

"I'm coming too," Bob said. "We can drink from the hose. There's one on their lawn." He whistled to Red, who came racing toward them, his long tongue hanging thirstily out of his mouth.

"Well, okay." She hadn't expected the whole gang to be with her.

Katie started across the street. She almost wished she hadn't mentioned calling her father. As she went up the curving flagstone path to the white front door, she felt sure there were eyes watching her from the large picture window. By the time she rang the chiming doorbell, the boys were crowded on the step behind her. She wished this were over.

The door opened after a minute, and Lynne stood there with Elizabeth and Sheryl behind her.

"Well, hello!" Lynne looked surprised. "What's going on?"

She glanced down at Jamie's suitcase. "Are you spending the night?" Her voice was amused.

Katie could feel her face flush. She realized they must be a strange-looking group, but it seemed too complicated to explain. "Well, uh, you see, Jamie got over here by mistake — "

"Look," Sheryl burst out. "He's got that ugly snake with him again."

Katie felt annoyed. George wasn't an ugly snake. He was just a snake, but this was no time for an argument. "Lynne, I wanted to know if I could use your phone to call my dad. Uh...the rest of them'll stay outside." She motioned toward the boys.

"It's there," Lynne said, pointing to a telephone in the front hall. "Don't you want to come in?" She smiled at the boys.

"No, that's okay," Will said. "Mind if we get a drink from your hose?"

"Why sure, but — " Before Lynne had a chance to say more, the boys had disappeared around the side of the house. Katie stepped into the hall.

"Is something wrong?" Sheryl asked. She was acting so important, it made Katie feel like a little girl.

"Well, not any more. We found Jamie, you see. I just have to call my dad." As Katie crossed the hall, she glanced into the living room. It was a long room, with a low-beamed ceiling, and it had yards and yards of luxurious white carpeting. How different *her* house was — old and brown-shingled, with what her mother said was sensible green carpeting in the living room. And sensible worn patches on the front lawn, too.

As Katie dialed her father's office number, she let her eyes roam over the spread of soft carpet. It was a good thing the boys didn't come in. She could just see their big brown footprints, like bear tracks, all over it.

"Hello." Thank heavens it was her father's deep voice!

"Oh, Dad!" she exclaimed.

"Katie, where have you been? I've been calling and calling."

"I'm sorry, Dad." Katie hurried into an account of the morning, hoping her father wouldn't be cross with her.

"Well," he said when she had finished, "I'm glad you found Jamie. Can you get back home now?" To her relief, he didn't scold her. She assured him they could and then hung up. When she turned back to the living room she saw the girls seated together on a wide curving sofa.

"Thank you, Lynne," Katie called into the living room. "Your house is beautiful." This burst from her lips without her even meaning to say it.

Lynne stood up. "Oh, that's okay." Her eyes were cool and unfriendly. Katie knew that Lynne must resent her being in the election.

The girls had obviously heard Katie's story on the phone, and so, apparently, had Lynne's mother, who was standing now in the hallway. "I'm glad you found your little brother," she said. "I guess you've had quite a time of it."

"Mama!" A little girl, with unsteady steps, came into the hall. She grabbed her mother's skirt and peered around at Katie with large blue eyes.

"Oh, she's a darling!" Katie exclaimed.

Mrs. Colby smiled with pleasure. She reached down to pick up the little girl, who hid on her mother's shoulder. Lynne's friends came into the hall and hovered around her, patting her hair and smiling at her.

"Thank you for letting me use the phone," said Katie. She opened the front door and there, sitting on the steps, were all the boys — Miller, his long legs stretched out before him; freckle-nosed Will; Bob Potter and Red; and Jamie, with his suitcase and snake. The bicycles were clustered together on the sidewalk.

"Oh." Mrs. Colby looked surprised. "I didn't realize anyone — "

Lynne came hurrying over to the door. It seemed to Katie that Lynne was pleased when everyone turned their attention away from her little sister. Katie wondered again if *she* would be jealous of a little sister.

"That's Katie's little brother, Mom. Remember, in the dress shop? And the others live near Katie," Lynne explained.

"Oh, why, yes. Hello." Mrs. Colby still seemed taken aback.

The boys got to their feet, and said thanks for the drink of water.

"But wouldn't you like a coke or something?" Lynne asked, smiling at the boys. Katie was afraid Jamie would say he was hungry and try to come in, so she hurried out the front door. Behind her, she heard Sheryl say, "Lynne, have you got a date to-night?"

"Sure, I have a date." Lynne laughed in a high voice. "We're going to that crazy party. Aren't you?"

Katie was impressed. Dates...parties...what would it be like? Once more she wondered how she had the nerve to run against a girl like Lynne Colby. Lynne already knew so many girls, and probably lots of the boys would vote for her too.

Katie thanked Mrs. Colby again and started down the walk behind the boys. Miller said he would take Jamie on his bike; Katie insisted on carrying George's box; and Bob slung Jamie's suitcase over the handlebars of his bike. Katie was just wondering whether she should go over and get on Will's bike when he called to her. "Come on, Katie." He beckoned her over.

"Oh, I can walk, Will," she said.

"Naw, come on! I'll give you a ride. I don't mind."

The girls were crowded in the doorway, listening.

"If he gets tired, I'll take you," Bob called over his shoulder as he wheeled down the street, balancing Jamie's suitcase.

"Come on, Katie," Will repeated.

Well, why not? Katie decided. It would be a lot

better than walking. Besides, Will could have ridden off and left her if he didn't want to give her a ride.

As Katie went toward him, she was aware that Lynne and her friends were still standing in the open doorway. She sat on the crossbar of Will's bike, and when he grabbed the handlebars and started to pedal, she felt very conscious of being practically enclosed in Will Madison's arms. She wished the girls would go back in the house and stop staring. Hadn't they ever seen a girl get a ride on a boy's bike before? It was just Will Madison, anyway.

Whispers

▲▲

On Tuesday Katie's mother and the new baby, Peter, came home from the hospital. Her mother looked so thin, after being so bulky all those months. She was smiling, and happy to be home. "Here, Katie," she said, when Katie got home from school that day, "do you want to hold Peter?" She placed the baby in Katie's arms.

Oh, what a red face! What a lot of soft, dark hair! And what tiny hands! Katie's heart gave a kind of lurch. She loved him. "He's cute, Mom. He's really cute — even if he is a *boy*." She laid her cheek next to his head for a minute and felt his warmth. Her baby brother. She saw a smile on her father's face. "He's really okay," she said to her father.

"Let me hold him," Jamie pleaded. "It's my turn."

It was wonderful to have Mom back home again. Katie and Dick and Jamie, too, were happy to help out. They washed the dishes at night and tried to be helpful in other ways, too.

Katie was so busy with things at home that she didn't notice what was happening at school. And it wasn't very noticeable at first. It was like being out in a boat on a smooth lake when suddenly the wind comes up. There is a ripple and another and another. But they are hardly noticeable until finally the boat is rocking up and down in the waves.

And thus Katie gradually realized something was wrong at school. Several times when she came up to a group of students in the hall, they seemed to change the subject of their conversation or suddenly stop talking all together. They would look at her with embarrassed faces. What was going on?

Thursday, the day before the election, Katie was turning a corner in the hall and almost bumped into Lynne and her friends. They were talking and laughing in high voices.

"Hello," Katie said, trying to be friendly.

"Oh, hi." Sheryl jerked around in surprise. Silence fell on the group which had been almost shrieking just the moment before. There was an awkward pause as every face turned toward Katie. She knew then that it wasn't her imagination; this sort of thing *had* been happening lately.

"Thanks again for letting me use your phone, Lynne," she said. Hers was the only voice in the entire hall.

"Oh...that's all right." Even the usually poised and controlled Lynne seemed flustered. She shook back her long dark hair. "How're your brothers?"

"Okay." Katie wished she knew what was going on. She decided to ask Sarah Lou if she had noticed anything, and walked off down the hall.

Then the same thing happened during noon recess when she stopped to talk to a group of classmates outside the school. When she was teasing Jeff about not making it for treasurer — he was the only one nominated for it — the girls in the group drifted awkwardly away and the boys looked embarrassed.

"You don't really think you're going to win, do you, Jeff?" Katie joked. Instead of laughing back at her, Jeff looked at her in the oddest way. And then he said:

"Are you going to win, Katie?"

"Well, if you vote for me." But what did he mean and why did he look so serious? As she walked away, those old doubts crept into her mind again. Maybe Lynne should get the job...Lynne again. Maybe Lynne should get the job...Lynne with her air of superiority.

"Katie!" It was Jody, followed by Sarah Lou and Mary. She was waving something and running across the crowded schoolyard toward Katie. She was frowning, and her eyes were darting about angrily. "Katie!" she shrieked. "I'm so mad! Look at this!" Jody shook a folded piece of notebook paper in front of Katie's face.

"What is it?" They all huddled around Jody.

"It's the worst thing." Jody kept shaking the paper. "Of all the mean, unfair —"

"Hold still." Katie steadied Jody's arm and began to read out loud: "Have you heard the latest about Katie Hart? It's all over school." Katie squinted at the rounded, scrawled writing. "They say she started the fire in the science room." And then in large printed letters it said: "FIREBUG! So we don't want *her* for president."

"Where did you find this?" Katie demanded.

"I found it in the girls' locker room, on the bench," Jody explained.

"That's rotten!" Sarah Lou said angrily.

Katie read the note again. She felt as though someone had slapped her. Standing there in the warm noonday sun, everything started to whirl around in the most sickening way. Was this what the kids were saying? Now she understood the whispers, the silences, the strange glances. It was frightening to be attacked this way. How could anyone be so mean?

"Oh," she gasped, tears filling her eyes. "What shall I do?"

"Don't cry, Katie." Her friends' arms were around her. "We know it's a big fat lie."

"Oh, it is! Just because I had to deliver notices that day —" She tried to hold back the tears. "Who wrote this awful thing?"

"It must be a girl," Mary declared, inspecting the paper. "That handwriting, and in the girls' locker room."

"I'll bet it's that Elm Garden crowd." Sarah Lou threw a suspicious glance around the playground. "They're trying to fix it so Lynne wins."

The bell rang, cutting through the noisy voices on the playground.

"Don't worry, Katie," Jody comforted her as they started slowly for the school building.

"I'd like to find out who did this." Katie frowned. "Should I go around asking who did it? If the other kids believe it, they'll vote for Lynne, for sure."

"No. Listen, Katie." Sarah Lou took the note. "We'll do it for you. That'd be better." She turned to the others. "Then we'll say how it's all a lie."

"You bet!" Jody agreed.

"Boy, I'd like to stop it," Katie said. "If we can."

But could anything be done before the election? Katie found it impossible to concentrate during her afternoon classes, except on this one sickening problem. Maybe she should go to Mr. Barker and tell him about the note? But she didn't want to. She felt like going right up to Lynne and asking her if she knew anything about it, but her mind shrank from such an encounter.

Mr. Schwartz called on her three times in social studies class before she answered, and then she hardly knew what she was saying. At the end of class, as she was gathering up her books, Will came over to her. "What's the matter, Katie? Something bothering you?"

She looked into Will's puzzled face. She didn't feel like any jokes — not even from Will. But he wasn't teasing. "Is something wrong?" he asked.

"Yes, there is," Katie admitted as they started for the hall. "Jody found a note in the girls' locker room. It said I started the fire in the science room and — and — not to vote for me." Katie held her hand over her lips to stop them from trembling.

"What." Will stared at her. She could feel her eyes beginning to sting. "Wow!" he said, his eyes seeming to darken. "You know, I heard some guys talking   "

The bell for the next class was ringing. "Of all the dirty tricks —" Katie was surprised by the anger in Will's voice. "Let's see the note," he demanded.

"Sarah Lou has it. She and Diane and Jody are trying to find out who wrote it."

"I'll bet I know." Will paused then added, "But what we really need to know is who started the fire."

"I wish I knew that, too," Katie said, wondering who the nameless, faceless person was who was letting her take the blame.

Paper Hearts

▲▲▲

That evening at the dinner table, Katie told her family about the note.

"What do you think I ought to do?" she asked.

"You could talk to Mr. Barker," her mother suggested. "It was a terrible thing to do. Do you want me to call him?"

"Oh, no, Mom. You know, he might come on the intercom and tell everybody about it. That would be really embarrassing."

The Harts continued to discuss the problem through dinner, but they didn't come to any solution that satisfied Katie.

After dinner Dick let Katie play his newest record, and Jamie offered to let her feed George.

Still, every time her mind swept back to school, she felt sick inside. She was being talked about and accused of something she hadn't done. It was a new and unpleasant experience.

Katie awoke the next morning with an uneasy feeling. She didn't want to face her classmates. It was a gray day outside, old brown leaves littered the sidewalk and the now-shabby lawns. As she opened her window she felt a chill in the air. She tried to enjoy the thought that it would be cold enough to wear her new green coat. She'd wear her new shoes, too. But even these didn't brighten her mood.

She dawdled in her room, watering two pots of ivy on her bureau, and then barely had time for breakfast before Dick and the boys were honking the horn out front.

"Wish I could stay home and help today," she said to her mother as she gathered up her books. Mrs. Hart was sitting in the old kitchen rocker, feeding Peter his bottle. She glanced about the kitchen, full of breakfast dishes.

"After school," she suggested. "Now you must go. Everything will turn out all right, dear. You'll see."

Katie knew her mother was trying to make her feel good. "Okay. Guess I'd better go then. Bye, Mom."

On the way to school, Jamie talked about Halloween. Will sat in the back with them, his school books stacked at his feet, and a large paper sack on his knees. When Jamie asked him what was in the sack, he brushed him off with a "nothing much, Jamie, just some stuff for school."

Up front, Dick and Chuck Miller and Bob Pot ter were discussing the weekend football game. Katie felt all alone. She shivered, despite the warmth of her new green coat. She'd be glad when this day was over.

When they reached the school, Will hurried off, and Katie made her way alone through the crowds in the halls. She caught sight of Maria up ahead and called to her. "Maria, wait for me." Katie expected Marie to turn around and flash her usual warm smile. But instead, when Maria's eyes lighted on Katie, an expression of — what was it, guilt? — came over her face. There was no smile. Maria turned without so much as a sign of greeting and plunged quickly into the crowd.

Katie was stunned. What could be the matter? She knew Maria had seen her. Why that strange look on her face?

"Katie!" Sarah Lou was coming down the hall. She pointed to a sign around her neck. It said: "Vote for Katie." Jody and Mary and Diane were wearing "Vote for Katie" signs too. How great it was to have friends! Katie put the puzzle about Maria out of her mind.

Then she saw Lynne. The Elm Garden girls, about a dozen of them, were gathered around her, hovering, admiring her outfit. As she shook back her long hair, Katie saw the glitter of little gold earrings, the kind that meant her ears had been pierced. All of Lynne's friends were wearing signs that said: "Vote for Lynne Colby." Katie was certain now that Lynne would win. There would be no meeting of class officers in Mr. Barker's office for Katie, no standing up in front of the big class meetings, no helping with the Valentine's Day dance.

"Hi, Lynne," Katie said, determined to be a good sport. Lynne's eyes took in Katie in such a cool way it made Katie feel small and insignificant.

"Hello, Katie." Lynne spoke carelessly. Then she turned back to her friends, who were still laughing. "And so I say, that *ees* wonderful. I like *eet* much." The other girls giggled at Lynne's accent, which Katie recognized immediately as an imitation of Maria's. "My, *eet ees* so *deeferent* here." Lynne's eyes flashed in a mocking way. She shook her hair so everyone could see her earrings, and everyone laughed again.

Anger began to burn deep inside Katie. Lynne

was making fun of Maria. "My name *ees* Maria," Lynne continued, trilling the "r" in Maria.

At that, everything went to pieces inside Katie. She walked over to Lynne. "Stop it!" she said angrily. "How would you like it if *you* were in a foreign country? How do you think you'd sound?" Katie's voice was loud and angry, even to her own surprised ears. She ignored the boys and girls who were passing by on all sides of them. "Why do you have to pick on a new girl, anyway?"

Lynne stared at her, her mouth hanging open. Katie whirled around then and walked back to her friends. The bell for the next class began jangling through the halls.

"That Lynne!" she said furiously. "Did you hear her? Making fun of Maria! Why does she *do* things like that?"

"I don't know," Diane frowned. "I notice she's nice enough to most of the kids — all except us. She's always waving and smiling at someone in the halls. Maybe she thinks she's being funny or something."

"Well, I wish she'd quit picking on Maria," Katie said. "Did you notice, she's had her ears pierced?"

"Oh, she would," Sarah Lou said with a shrug. "Anyway, I'm glad you told her off."

But Katie was having second thoughts about

that. Maybe she shouldn't have lost her temper that way. But wouldn't it have been worse not to speak up at all?

Katie agreed to meet her friends in the cafeteria at lunchtime, then hurried through the crowded halls to her locker. She passed groups of boys and girls carrying small red paper hearts, and she noticed several paper hearts on the floor in front of the lockers. It's the wrong time of year for valentines, she thought.

"Hey, look!" someone yelled out. "I got one too."

"Me too," someone else called out. Suddenly everywhere Katie looked she saw students with red paper hearts.

Confession

▲▲

Katie pulled open the door of her locker and there, down among her books, lay one of the paper hearts. Someone had slipped it through the slot in the door. Katie picked it up and examined it — a plain red paper heart, the kind she made every Valentine's Day. "Look at that!" she exclaimed out loud.

"Pretty smart, Katie," the boy who had the next locker said to her.

"Why, yes — wow! What a fantastic idea! I guess my friends must have done it."

"They're trying to help you — you know, after all that talk —" He broke off suddenly, and hurried away down the hall.

73

Did everybody in the whole school know about it? That gossip — that awful gossip! Katie started back through the halls. There were red hearts scattered up and down the floor, little patches of bright red everywhere. She couldn't help smiling. But how had Sarah Lou managed to keep such a secret from her? Usually Sarah Lou told Katie everything.

When class ended, Katie rushed out of the room to look for her friends. Going through the crowded hall, she saw Maria up ahead and this time she was determined to catch up with her. "Maria!" she called. Maria turned around. Her dark eyes looked frightened and she did not smile, but she didn't run away. "Maria, what's the matter?"

"Oh, Katie." She pressed her hand over her mouth. There were tears in her eyes.

"Maria, tell me. What's wrong?" Other students crowded past, nudging them from all sides. Katie pulled Maria into an empty classroom. "Can I help you?"

"No, no. *I* must help you."

"What do you mean?" But Maria shook her head. The tears shone in her eyes. "Please, tell me, Maria."

Maria took a deep breath. "Okay, then. I tell you. Today I hear the Elm girls say you start the fire in the science room. I know that is not true

because," her whole face quivered, "I think I start the fire."

Katie stared in amazement. "You?"

"I was in there. I was working on an experiment with a Bunsen burner. I hear the bell ring for the next class and I run out. I think maybe I knock the burner over when I pick up my books."

"But why didn't you tell Mr. Barker?" Katie asked.

"He maybe says I can't come to this school. I can't tell him. But now I must tell him to save you. What can I do?" Maria twisted her hands nervously.

Katie put her arm around her friend. "Don't worry about saving me, Maria. My friends don't believe that talk. And I know Mr. Barker doesn't either. But it would be better if you tell Mr. Barker before he finds out. He won't make you leave school. Really, it won't be too bad."

"Oh, but I am afraid. I know you are right, but —" Maria broke off and looked more frightened than ever.

The bell would be ringing soon for the next class. "Listen, Maria," Katie urged, "I'll go with you to the office. Would that help?"

"Oh, Katie. If — if you would —"

"You'll feel a lot better after you talk to Mr. Barker. Really, you will." Katie took Maria's arm and started her toward the office. "It won't be that bad, honest. You can explain it all to him."

"Now they will all know about me, what I did. All the students will know. What will they say?" Maria's voice quavered.

"Look, Maria, maybe they won't have to know." Katie knew how it felt to be talked about. "I promise I won't tell —" *Even if it meant clearing yourself?* a little voice inside her asked. *Right*, she said to the voice. She certainly wouldn't go around telling on Maria.

Maria stopped at the office door. "Katie, I heard about what you say to Lynne this morning. Thank you. If they come to my country, maybe we laugh at them, too."

So Maria knew about her outburst at Lynne. Had she heard the Elm Garden gang mocking her? "Forget about them," Katie said. "Let's go in."

"Katie, I can do it now." Maria opened the office door. "I go in alone. Thank you, Katie." She smiled a little and closed the door behind her.

Poor Maria, worrying all this time. How hard it must be for her — in a new country with a new language, all new friends, everything different. If she'd only told Mr. Barker in the beginning....

Katie hurried to her next class. She noticed there were more paper hearts on the floor, and again she wondered how Sarah Lou could have kept such a secret. Katie rounded the corner and rushed into math class as the last bell was ringing.

There was just time to turn in her seat and whisper to Sarah Lou behind her. "Thanks for the paper hearts."

"Don't thank me," Sarah Lou whispered back. "I didn't do it."

Katie looked at her in astonishment.

"Class, quiet, please," the teacher said. "I'm going to pass out the ballots for the election before class starts. Mark them, fold them, and pass them forward. We have only a few minutes for this. So, please, hurry. The results will be posted after school."

White pieces of paper were fluttering down the rows from hand to hand. The time had come at last.

Katie spread the ballot in front of her. She checked the names she wanted for vice president, secretary, and Jeff for treasurer, of course. Then she came to a halt: Lynne Colby or Katie Hart for president. Was it right to vote for yourself? As if she could see right into Katie's mind, Sarah Lou jabbed her between the shoulder blades.

Katie marked her own name. It wouldn't be fair to her friends and it wouldn't make sense to throw away one whole vote. She looked up at the hands on the clock. How slowly they jumped from minute to minute, moving forward at last to the end of the election.

"You and Your Boys"

▲▲▲

The cafeteria was crowded. Everyone was talking and laughing. Some students Katie knew, and some she didn't, called out, "Good luck! Hope you win, Katie." As the lunch hour passed, she felt more and more excited and hopeful, and a little puzzled. She found out that Diane, Mary, and Jody hadn't passed out the red hearts either.

In the afternoon as she was going through the halls between classes, she met Will. His eyes lighted up at the sight of her. "Katie," he said as he grabbed her by the arm, "I found out about the note. The other kids think that fire talk was a dirty trick. They don't believe it."

"Honest? Really?" She stared at Will. So maybe

it wouldn't help Lynne after all. "Thanks for telling me, Will." She went into class smiling to herself, thinking how nice that was of him. Some of the students in the room waved red paper hearts at her.

It felt good to get to PE at the end of the day. Katie pounded the volleyball and laughed and shouted with the others. She relaxed and felt better about the note and about Maria, too. Then physical education was over. She was back in the locker room and it was time for the results!

"Come on, Sarah Lou." Katie wanted to get down to the office and know the outcome. She was tired of waiting. She and Sarah Lou raced down the hall to the bulletin board. The students grouped around it called out, "They don't know yet. They aren't through counting." Katie saw Will in the big crowd that was jostling around in front of the principal's office.

"Oh, no!" Sarah Lou exclaimed. "More waiting."

Katie suddenly remembered that she had left her coat in the locker room. "Listen, Sarah Lou, you wait here, okay? I'll be back in a minute. I forgot my coat." She hurried down the hall again, afraid the room might already be locked.

But the door whooshed open when she pushed it.

She ran past a long row of gray lockers. Someone was sitting on one of the benches at the back of the room, long dark hair falling over her face. "Lynne!" Katie slid to a halt and Lynne looked up, startled.

"Oh, it's you." Lynne tried to spread her hands over her lap, but Katie could see the pile of red paper hearts, all torn to pieces.

"What are you doing *here*?" Katie asked.

Lynne shook back her hair, so that her earrings glinted in the light. She stood up, clutching the handful of red paper, and walked over to a trash can, and dropped it in. "You'll probably win, you know," she said bitterly. "You and your valentines."

"Do you think so? With everyone talking about the fire? And that note —" Katie broke off, just short of making an accusation.

"Oh...that." Lynne looked a little embarrassed now. "I'm sorry about that. Sheryl did it. I told her to stop, when I found out. It was dumb. We knew you didn't start it, and trying to blame it on you...that made a lot of the kids mad at us."

So it was Sheryl. Katie should have known the other kids would see through it, and resent it.

"But everything works out for you." Lynne's tone was bitter. "You and your boys."

"What do you mean, me and my boys?" Katie

was so startled she could only stare at Lynne.

"You know what I mean. They take you around on their bikes...drive you in their car...help you win elections." Lynne threw this last comment over her shoulder as she turned toward the door.

Katie had never looked at it this way before. Hearing herself described this way, she could finally understand Lynne. It probably looked pretty good to her, having an older brother's car to ride around in, and Will and the others helping her out. She thought of that day at Lynne's house.

"Say, Lynne, wait!" Katie hurried after her. "You want to know something? I always thought *you* were the lucky one."

Lynne paused at the door and turned her dark eyes on Katie. "Me?"

"Yes, you. You have all those friends where you live and — and a really nice house with a white rug — " Katie knew that must sound dumb "— and a little sister —"

"Little sister!" Lynne echoed. "She's all my parents ever think about. If I win, maybe they'll stop thinking about her for once. Oh, but I won't. Not with those boys running around helping you."

"What boys helping me? What you talking about? Besides, you have *dates* with boys."

"Oh, that..." Lynne pushed the door open quickly. "We just made that up," she mumbled, tossing her hair over her shoulders again and walking out of the locker room. The door swung shut behind her.

Katie stood in the silent room and stared after her. Lynne Colby envied her. Lynne was jealous of her own little sister...she pretended she had dates...she envied Katie because of her brother and his friends. If she only knew they were around most of the time because they wanted to be with Dick and his car.

Katie went back to pick up her coat. She walked through the quiet locker room, thinking about Lynne. Those paper hearts had really upset her.

Katie hurried back down the hall to the crowd by the bulletin board. As she approached, Mr. Barker's secretary was coming out of the office to tack up the results of the election on the bulletin board. Time to find out now. Time at last!

Everyone squeezed forward to read the paper. Then a wild squeal of joy went up, then another, and another. The Elm Garden girls pushed forward into a knot around Lynne!

Katie stepped back, away from the noise and the voices. She felt a sudden emptiness in her stomach. She had lost! But she'd known she would all the time, hadn't she? Suddenly Katie realized how much she had let herself get to hoping. The Elm Garden crowd were jumping all around

Lynne, hugging her, shouting and yelling. Katie caught a glimpse of Lynne's face, happy, smiling, flushed — so different from the bitter face she'd seen in the locker room a few minutes ago.

A group of Katie's friends came toward her. They swooped around her, hugging her. Quick tears stung Katie's eyes. Sarah Lou was crying. "Katie, she won, isn't it terrible?" Sarah Lou sobbed. Mary was wiping her eyes, too. It seemed like a funeral. Oh, it hurt, it really hurt. There was no use pretending it didn't.

"It's okay," she said to them. "We sort of guessed Lynne would win, didn't we? It's all right. She's older and she's done more, and a lot of people know her."

"Oh, Katie, but I was hoping —" Sarah Lou wept.

"It's not fair," Diane said.

"Yes, it is." Katie had to smile at them. "It's only an election, you know. Did she win by much?"

"A hundred and fifty-three to a hundred and forty-one." Sarah Lou made a face. "Really close."

"A hundred and forty-one!" Katie stared at Sarah Lou. "I got that many votes? Fantastic!"

"I wish you got more," Maria said.

"I do too." Katie smiled at Maria. Then she

hugged her and whispered in her ear. "Is everything okay?"

Maria whispered back, "Okay. *Bueno!*"

Now more students were pressing around them. "Good try, Katie," they called out. "It was a close one."

"Katie." Jeff pushed through the crowd to her side. "Don't feel too bad. A lot of kids say you ought to try again next year. If you'd only had a little more time. That note was a rotten trick."

Jeff's face was friendly and his words helped soothe the hurt. But now, she knew, she must do the right thing. She started toward Lynne and her group.

"Lynne," she called. The others stepped back. "Congratulations." Lynne looked at her, the smile fading from her face. "Good luck," Katie added.

Lynne's face flushed a little, as if she wasn't sure how to behave. "Thanks. Katie, I wanted to ask you — I was hoping —" Her voice faltered for a moment. "I was hoping you and — and Maria would be on the dance committee."

Katie stared at her. Lynne wanted them to be on her dance committee? Maybe she was improving already. "Sure. I'd like to," Katie smiled. "But you'll have to ask Maria."

And now Katie wanted to leave. She started down the hall with her closest friends. Dick's jam-packed car was waiting in the parking lot. Will was already leaning against it. Jamie was in the back seat.

"Can you come over, Katie?" Sarah Lou asked.

"No, I have to go home and help Mom." And in a way she was glad to go home and have something else to think about. She started toward the car.

"Hi, Dick. Hi, Miller."

"Pretty tough, Katie. Will told us." Dick gave her a smile.

Katie climbed into the back seat, and Will squeezed in beside her.

"I'm sorry you lost, Katie," Jamie said, patting her arm.

"I know, Jamie. Thanks."

Katie noticed, as they pulled out of the parking lot, that Lynne and her crowd were standing on the sidewalk in front of the school.

Suddenly she remembered about the paper hearts. She turned to Will. "You know those valentine hearts?" she said. There was something about his look, the way he was smiling at her.

"What about them?" he asked.

"Well, it was a great idea and —"

"I thought you'd figure it out."

"Will! You *did* do it!" Will had helped her in the election! "You went around and put them in the lockers? Oh, wow!"

Katie tipped her face up into the afternoon sunshine. That's what Lynne Colby meant, all that talk about "you and your boys."

"Thanks, Will," Katie said to the sun. "Thanks ever so much." She turned her head a little. A red flush was creeping up Will's neck and over his face.

"It was nothing," he said in a pleased, hoarse voice. "Just some old valentines. Tough luck you didn't win. It was close, though."

"Valentines!" Jamie shouted. "What're you two talking about valentines for? We haven't even had Halloween yet."

Katie laughed, and then said very thoughtfully, "You know, since the election was so close I think I'll try again."

"You should, Katie," Will urged her. "I think you'd win next time. And I'll help you." His blue eyes were smiling at her. He seemed to like the idea a lot...or maybe he liked her.

"Okay." Katie smiled back at him. She realized that Lynne had been right. She was very lucky. She knew that now for sure.